To Pastor Cathy!
Reach the Beach!
Irma Vitey

Sandy Vitey

Kaitlyn

Zak

Sam

# Our Favorite Time Of The Year

By Imre, Sandy, Kaitlyn, Zachary and Samuel Vitez

Published by Sand Dreams™ Press, LLC
P.O. Box 24
Whitehouse Station, New Jersey
08889-0024,
United States of America

www.sanddreamspress.com

Printed in Hong Kong through Bolton Associates, Inc.,
San Rafael, California

Printed on paper certified to be originating
from sustainable forests.

All photographs taken by the authors except:
beach bungalow by Francis and Vilma Vitez,
and family beach portrait by Kristina Poznan.

Special thanks to Margaret.

ISBN: 978-0-9798656-0-2

# Dedication

*Our Favorite Time Of The Year* is dedicated to the John, Filep, Neely and Vitez families
who first took us on summer vacations to beach bungalows at the sea shore.
As years pass, children become adults and take their children down the shore,
allowing them to also experience wonderful summers at the beach.

This book is based upon our summers on Long Beach Island, an 18-mile-long island
on the New Jersey coastline, situated between Sandy Hook and Cape May.
Our family, like many other families on vacation at the shore,
spends most of our time searching for perfect sea shells, wave jumping,
making sand castles, feeding sea gulls, and watching sunsets.

These are the things that make summer "our favorite time of the year!"

Imre, Sandy, Kaitlyn, Zachary and Samuel Vitez

# Glossary

Begin your vacation by reviewing these words and maps to familiarize yourselves with the seashore. Look for these words and photographs of these items as you read the story.

**bay:**          A body of calm water between two land masses.

**blue claws:**    A type of crab you can catch in the bay.

**causeway:**     A bridge or raised road between the mainland and an island.

**inlet:**          An opening between islands through which boats can pass from the bay to the ocean.

**island:**         A small land mass surrounded by water.

**jetty:**         A line of large rocks that protect the shoreline.

**jump waves:**  When you stand at the edge of the ocean looking for a wave to dive into.

**lighthouse:**   A building having a strong light at the top to warn ships of the coast line.

**mainland:**     The larger body of land beside a smaller island.

**sea gulls:**    The white and grey colored birds usually seen near the seashore.

**seashore:**     An area where the ocean meets the land, often covered with sand or rocks.

**seaweed:**      The plant life found growing in the water.

**seining:**       Use of a net to catch fish in the bay or the ocean.

**ocean:**        A very large body of salt water.

**tide pool:**    A small pond of water that is often created in the sand when the tide is low.

**waves:**         The water that rolls in from the ocean onto the shore.

# Maps

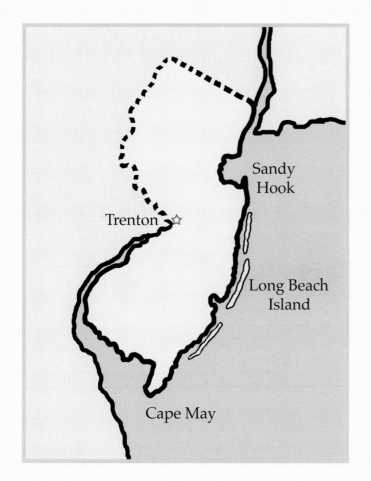

New Jersey

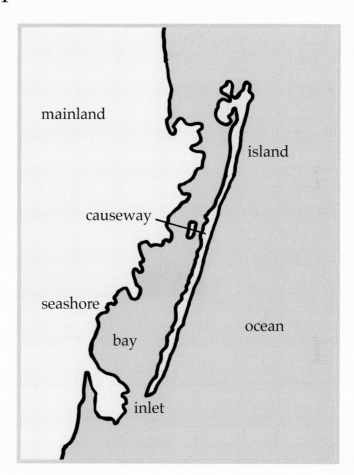

Long Beach Island

Our favorite time of the year is when we go on vacation to Long Beach Island.

When we arrive, the first thing we do is
say hello to the lighthouse at Barnegat Light.

While waiting to go into our beach house,
we play in the tide pools,

and go rock climbing on the jetties.

We get so excited
that we want to
run to get into
the water,

... and sometimes we can't get ourselves out of the sand.

In the morning, we love to go jumping in
the big ocean waves,

and later in the day when we're tired,
we like to float in the calm waters at the bay beach.

If we're just learning how to boogie-board,
we can first practice on land,

or we can simply relax in the water.

We never know if we have the
right mix of sand and water,

to build sand castles all day long.

We need to keep the seaweed out of the
way while seining for small fish,

or use it to keep cool in the heat of the day.

When we're on vacation, we can have ice cream at least twice a day!

Sometimes
snuggling with
your Mom
is the best!

We need to have a lot of patience, when we're trying to catch blue claw crabs,

and when we're fixing
the gold medal catch for dinner.

We always find time to practice our golf swing when we are down the shore.

We also like to ride the wild ponies
at the amusement park.

Later in the day, we like to watch the
fishing boats coming into the inlet.

The beach is a great place to share secrets with a special friend.

When there is no one on the beach on a cloudy day, it's fun to go digging in the sand,

or to feed the sea gulls.

When the sun is getting ready to set, we check the bay one last time,

and say good night to Barnegat Light.

Our family will
always remember
our vacations on
Long Beach Island.